Dangerous Double Dare!

"I think you're bluffing!" Stephanie said. "You're a scaredy cat—just like your dog!"

"Baby's not a scaredy cat!" Missy said.

"If you're so brave, why don't you prove it on Halloween? You can spend the midnight hour inside the Rochester House," said Stephanie.

"Oooh!" Emily squealed. "I would never do that! Anything can happen inside a haunted house, especially on Halloween!"

"Or, are you a chicken, just like your dog?" Stephanie asked. "You can take him with you, but I don't think he'll give you much protection."

"Baby's a good watchdog," Missy said, starting to feel a sharp twinge in her stomach.

"So then it's settled." Stephanie crossed her arms and gave Missy a smile. "On Halloween night Missy has a date—with a ghost!"

FRIGHT NIGHT

by Molly Albright

illustrated by Eulala Conner

Troll Associates

Library of Congress Cataloging-in-Publication Data

Albright, Molly.
   Fright night / by Molly Albright; illustrated by Eulala Conner.
     p.   cm.
   Summary: Missy accepts a challenge from Stephanie to spend
Halloween night with her dog in a haunted house.
   ISBN 0-8167-1486-X (lib. bdg.)   ISBN 0-8167-1487-8 (pbk.)
   [1. Haunted houses—Fiction. 2. Halloween—Fiction.] I. Conner,
Eulala, ill. II. Title.
PZ7.A325Fr 1989
[Fic]—dc19   88-12388

A TROLL BOOK, published by Troll Associates,
Mahwah, NJ 07430

Copyright © 1989 by Troll Associates, Mahwah, New Jersey

Printed in the United States of America.

10 9 8 7 6 5 4 3 2 1

FRIGHT NIGHT

CHAPTER

1

———

The room was dimly lit and dancing with shadows. The house was completely silent. From its spot on Melissa's dresser, a jack-o'-lantern cast a ghostly glow over the girls' faces.

"And then," Willie whispered, "Three-Fingered Aggie reached out and grabbed her!"

The girls gasped in unison.

"Oh my gosh!" Melissa Fremont exclaimed. Baby, her Old English sheepdog, let out a bark. Missy patted him on the back to quiet him down. "It's okay, Baby," she whispered. "And the girl was all alone in the graveyard?" Missy asked Willie.

Willie nodded, her eyes glimmering. "Pretty scary, isn't it?" Fun-loving Wilhelmina Wagnalls was a convincing storyteller.

"And then what happened?" Emily Green asked. "What did Three-Fingered Aggie do to her?"

"Well," Willie continued, "it was terrible. The girl tried to get away, but—"

"*Owwyouuuu!*" Baby howled suddenly, making all the girls jump with fright.

"Would you make that stupid dog of yours shut up?" Stephanie Cook snapped at Missy. "He almost made me spill my cider."

"Baby's not stupid," Missy said over the dog's howling. "He's just upset because you're sitting on his tail. You're hurting him."

"Fat chance!" Stephanie said, moving away from the big fluffy sheepdog.

Baby's howl faded to a whimper as Missy patted his head. Melissa enjoyed throwing sleepover parties for her friends, but sometimes things got a little crazy. For one thing, Stephanie and Baby didn't get along too well, and often it was up to Missy to keep the peace.

So far, the party had been a success. The girls had bobbed for apples and designed their group Halloween costume before curling up in their sleeping bags to tell scary stories.

"Will you please finish the story?" Emily begged. "I'm dying of curiosity!"

"To this day, no one really knows the horrible things Three-Fingered Aggie did to the poor girl in the graveyard that Halloween night," Willie said. "But the next morning, when the other kids came back, they found

the girl at the foot of Three-Fingered Aggie's statue. Stone cold dead!"

"Oooh!" Emily shivered. "Killed by the ghost of Three-Fingered Aggie!"

Willie lowered her voice to a somber tone. "At the base of the statue, they found the message: *Dare not, die not!* And Three-Fingered Aggie was wearing a chain of daisies around her neck. But her arms were outstretched . . . waiting . . . hoping for her next victim!"

"Oooh!" The girls gasped in horror.

"After that," Willie continued, "the statue of Three-Fingered Aggie disappeared from the graveyard. No one knows where it went . . . or where it will turn up next!"

"That's what happens when you mess with ghosts," Stephanie said seriously. "Imagine, spending Halloween night in a graveyard. That girl was nuts!"

"I'll bet the girl just died of fright," Missy said, trying to think of a logical explanation for the ghost story. "And maybe her parents took the statue out of the graveyard so that it would never scare or hurt anyone again."

Stephanie gave her a stony look. "Missy, are you kidding me? Don't tell me you don't believe in ghosts!"

Missy shrugged. "It's a pretty spooky story, Willie. And what's a Halloween party without a few ghost stories?"

Baby barked in agreement.

Stephanie huddled into her sleeping bag.

"Boy, am I glad we don't have any graveyards in this neighborhood."

"Yeah," Emily added. "It would be pretty creepy if you had to pass all those tombstones every time you walked down the street."

"Wait a minute!" Willie chimed in. "You may not have a cemetery near here, but there's a haunted house in my neighborhood—right down the street from my house!"

Willie lived on the other side of the park that was at the end of Missy and Stephanie's street.

"Really?" Stephanie's eyes lit up with interest.

Willie nodded. "The old Rochester house. Maybe we should check it out sometime."

"I know that house," Stephanie said. "It definitely looks like it could be haunted."

"Maybe we should turn the lights back on," Emily suggested. "This is getting creepy."

"Maybe we would run into the ghost of old Mrs. Rochester . . ." Stephanie continued.

"Maybe we should quit with the ghost stories," Emily said. She twisted her long dark ponytail nervously around her fingers.

"Maybe her ghost will reach out and grab one of us, then—"

Suddenly the room went pitch-black, and everyone screamed.

"It's the ghost of old Mrs. Rochester!" Willie shouted.

"It's just the jack-o'-lantern, silly," Missy answered. "The candle probably burned out."

Baby started barking, and before Missy could stop him, he dove out of her arms.

"Help!" Stephanie shrieked. "I'm being trampled by a giant monster!"

"It's her, I tell you! It's the ghost of Mrs. Rochester!" shouted Willie.

"Somebody turn on the lights!" Emily cried.

The overhead light flicked on, revealing Missy's safe, normal bedroom. Aside from the sprawl of tangled sleeping bags and four very excited girls, there was nothing out of the ordinary, nothing to fear, no ghosts in the air.

"Some party," Missy's father remarked from the doorway.

"Would you get this mutt off me!" Stephanie shrieked. She was pinned under Baby. "Yuck!" she squealed as his wet nose touched her cheek.

"Some monster." Missy pulled her dog away from her angry friend. "I guess Baby was just trying to save you from the ghost of old Mrs. Rochester," Missy said with a chuckle.

"Blech! Dog germs!" Stephanie rubbed her cheek hard.

The other girls covered their mouths, trying to hold back an explosion of giggles.

"I was looking for my daughter's Halloween party," said Mr. Fremont. "When I heard the screams, I knew I was in the right place." He smiled at Missy and her friends. Beside him stood two men and a pretty red-haired young woman. They were all dressed in formal clothes, the uniform of musicians in the Indian-apolis Symphony. Mr. Fremont played first viola with the symphony.

Missy smiled at them. "We were telling scary stories," she explained, "and the candle burned out."

"I'm telling you, it was Old Lady Rochester's ghost," Willie insisted, her eyes twinkling.

Missy was beginning to wonder if Willie had blown the candle out just to scare them.

"Ghosts, eh?" Missy's father said. "Guess we really have a full house tonight." He nodded toward the other adults. "I brought some of the new musicians home after our concert for a glass of apple cider. They wanted to meet you."

The red-haired woman stepped forward and poked her head into Missy's bedroom. "Did I hear you girls talking about ghosts and haunted houses?"

"We were just joking around," Emily explained.

"About the old Rochester mansion," Willie added.

"I see," the woman said, smiling. "But you'd better be careful when joking about the spirit world." She lifted her eyebrows, teasing the girls. "The spirits could come back to haunt you!"

"Oooh!" Emily said with a shiver.

"See?" Stephanie cried. "I told you this stuff is real, Missy."

"Who wants hot cider?" Mrs. Fremont called from the hallway.

"Have fun, girls," one of the musicians called as the adults filed past the bedroom door, heading toward the living room.

Just then, Missy's mother appeared with a tray of candy apples. "I brought you a Halloween treat," she said.

"Thanks, Mom." Missy had helped her mother dip apples in melted caramel sauce earlier that day.

"But I do hope the seance is over," Mrs. Fremont teased. "Such commotion! You know the old saying: Let sleeping dogs lie."

As if on cue, Baby bounded over to her and nuzzled against her leg. Mrs. Fremont tousled the dog's fur, then returned to her guests.

"Speaking of sleeping dogs," Stephanie said, "don't you think it's time to put that dog of yours outside for the night?"

"Baby?" Missy asked. "But he always sleeps in here—with me."

"Gross!" Stephanie groaned.

Emily reached out and patted Baby's hefty flank. "Oh, come on, Stephanie. He's not *that* bad." She grinned. "Just huge."

Baby padded back over to Missy. She put her arms around her sheepdog's neck and hugged him. Baby *was* enormous now, but Missy remembered when he had been just a tiny shaggy puppy. She had chosen Baby, just as Missy's parents had chosen her, when she was a tiny baby waiting to be adopted.

Although Missy was glad that she'd made friends since her family had moved to Indianapolis, Baby was still her best friend in the whole world. He'd stuck with her through thick and thin, through all the tough moments when Missy had wondered if she would ever be happy in her new home.

Stephanie looked at the big sheepdog and sighed. "Well, I guess I should get used to having a dog around. My cousin Peter and his poodle, Fifi, are coming to visit. They'll be staying with me for a few weeks."

Missy's face lit up with a grin. "I didn't even know you had a cousin named Peter, Stephanie."

"Is he cute?" Willie asked.

"Absolutely adorable," Stephanie said, flipping a strand of silky blond hair over her shoulder. "But what would you expect? He *is* related to me, you know."

Willie nudged Missy and whispered, "Modest, isn't she?"

"Come on, Steph," Emily prodded. "Tell us all about him."

"What do you want to know?" asked Stephanie.

Willie jumped up and grabbed a caramel apple. "How old is he?"

"What grade is he in?" Missy added.

"Does he play with frogs and all the other gross things that boys like?" asked Emily.

"Of course not," Stephanie snapped. "No cousin of mine would be so disgusting! Besides, Peter is only three years old."

"In that case," Missy said with a sigh, "maybe you'd better tell us about Fifi."

"She's a toy French poodle," Stephanie explained as she straightened the lacy sleeve of her nightgown. "A pedigree. My aunt and uncle are leaving Fifi and Peter with us while they visit Europe."

"You're going to be stuck with a three-year-old twerp?" Willie moaned. "Good luck."

"Peter is not a twerp," insisted Stephanie. "He's a perfect angel."

"If he's so perfect, why don't his parents take him along?" Missy asked.

"'Cause he's a little kid, silly." Stephanie went over to the night stand and picked up a shiny candied apple. "Just wait till you see Fifi. She's the cutest, most well-trained toy poodle in the whole world." She looked down just in time to see Baby sniff at Missy's mug of spiced apple cider. "Fifi's not at all like your overgrown horse of a dog. In fact, you'd better keep Baby locked up. He'll scare Fifi."

"If Fifi's just a toy, how could Baby scare her?" Emily asked.

"Emily Green, don't you know anything?" Stephanie said huffily. She knelt down on the rug and daintily bit into her apple.

Willie giggled. "*Toy* poodle just means that it's small. The kind of dog that Baby could gobble up as a snack." She took a big bite of her candy apple.

"Baby would never do that. He's a gentle

dog. Right, pal?" Missy buried her face in Baby's furry neck.

"I mean it, Missy." Stephanie wagged the apple over her shoulder as if she were going to throw it at Missy. "You'd better keep that mongrel away from Fifi. You'd better . . . ouch!" she yelped. Her candy apple had gotten tangled in some strands of her long hair.

"Trapped in her own hair," Willie commented as she swallowed a mouthful of apple.

"Help me!" Stephanie wailed. "I'm stuck!" She pulled at the apple, trying to free her hair.

"Don't do that," Emily said, rushing over to Stephanie. "You're making it worse!"

"What should I do?" Stephanie whined.

The girls stood clustered around their friend, examining the tangle. Baby nosed his way into the circle. He hated to be left out.

"*Ahhhrrr!*" Stephanie groaned. "I'm getting all sticky!"

"Maybe we should cut it out," Willie suggested.

"No!" A fat tear rolled down Stephanie's cheek, and Baby lurched forward to lick it away.

"That's a boy." Missy patted Baby.

"Get him away from me!" Stephanie cried, shoving the dog back.

But it was too late. When he brushed against Stephanie, Baby had leaned against the sticky mess. His fur was now glued to Stephanie's hair.

"Baby's stuck too!" Emily exclaimed.

Missy dashed to her desk and found a pair of scissors. But when she returned to the glued-together twosome, she wasn't quite sure how to begin. "Yuck!"

"What do you mean, yuck?" Stephanie said in a shrill voice. "I'm glued to this mangy mongrel and all you can say is yuck?"

"It's pretty gross from this angle too," Willie said, taking the scissors from Missy. "Now, hold still."

With a few careful snips Stephanie, Baby, and the sticky apple were free.

Stephanie touched her hair. "Ouch!" she screeched. "I have a bald spot! I can feel it!"

Willie handed the hairy apple to Missy, who inspected it for a moment. Then she wrapped the apple in some paper towels and dropped it into her wastepaper basket.

"My hair is ruined! Thanks to that—that dog!"

Missy smiled weakly at Stephanie. "Sorry."

Stephanie ran to the mirror to survey the damage. "Oooh, I can't wait till Fifi gets here. Then you'll see how a polite dog behaves."

Emily patted her on the back. "Don't worry. It'll grow out."

Willie held up the shiny silver scissors and snipped at the air. "Who's next for a trim?"

CHAPTER

2

On Monday morning Stephanie barely nodded in Missy's direction when they met at the bus stop. Missy sighed. She wondered if her friend was still upset over losing a clump of her hair to a candy apple.

When the bus arrived, Stephanie stomped to the back, a scowl on her face.

"What's the matter with you?" Emily asked as Stephanie slid into the seat beside her.

"Everything." Stephanie folded her arms over her backpack and stared straight ahead.

Emily turned around to talk to Missy. "What's wrong? Did you two have a fight?"

"No. I think she's just being grumpy," Missy said.

"I am not a grump, and I don't like you

talking about me as if I'm not even here," Stephanie complained.

Emily eyed her friend cautiously. "Looks like someone got up on the wrong side of the bed this morning."

"*Someone* was woken up at five-thirty in the morning." Stephanie's lips curled into a pout. "Peter showed up yesterday. I don't understand it. He used to be such a little doll, following me around without a peep." She sighed. "Now he's a living terror."

Emily and Missy both giggled.

"It's not funny," Stephanie insisted. "I was sound asleep, when I heard this rattling noise. I opened my eyes and Peter was standing there, shaking his plastic piggy bank over my head. He kept saying, 'Pennies! I want pennies!' "

Missy smiled. "I guess Peter the angel has grown into a little devil."

The bus stopped again and Willie climbed aboard. "What's going on?" she asked, plopping into the seat next to Missy.

"Peter the adorable arrived yesterday," Missy answered.

"More like Peter the horrible," Emily added.

Willie grinned. "So he isn't a perfect angel anymore, huh?"

Stephanie sighed and leaned back. "I just don't understand it . . ."

"How's Fifi?" Willie asked.

Stephanie smiled, cheering up a bit. "At least Fifi is still adorable. You've got to see her. She has cute little red bows tied all over her fur, and her tail is clipped into a tiny little pompom at the end."

"Bows?" Missy asked. "Don't they get in her way?"

"Of course not," Stephanie said. "Poodles are very dainty and ladylike. Why don't you all come over after school today? We can work on our Halloween costumes, and you can meet Fifi—and Peter, too, I guess."

Everyone nodded. Fifi sounded cute, and Peter sounded like a sight to behold.

Stephanie Cook lived in a big white two-story house right across the street from Missy's one-story ranch-style house. After school, as the girls walked up the steps, the front door popped open and a white poodle ran out. A second later, a small blond boy emerged, chasing after the dog.

"Hi, Peter! Hi, Fifi!" Stephanie called, running up the steps ahead of the other girls. She tried to grab Fifi, but the poodle yapped and edged away from her. Instead, she turned to Peter and gave him a reluctant hug.

"Stop it, Steph!" Peter squirmed out of her arms and scrambled down the steps toward the nervous dog. "Fifi! Come to PeeWee!"

The little poodle eyed him suspiciously but stood its ground, quivering in the cool October air.

"PeeWee?" Willie repeated with a smirk.

"I know it sounds silly," Stephanie muttered. "He can't say Petey, so that's what he calls himself. He's only three."

"There you are." Mrs. Cook appeared at the door, a relieved look on her face. "I'm glad you're home, Stephanie. I need to rest for a while. I'm not used to small boys and dogs." Her usually perfect hair was mussed, and she had a large stain on her blouse.

"Okay, Mom." As the girls filed into the house, Fifi barked twice and leapt into Peter's arms.

"Wait for PeeWee!" the young boy shouted to the girls.

Stephanie winced. "I liked it better before, when he couldn't talk yet."

When everyone was settled in the family room, Stephanie's mother started up the stairs. "Try to keep you-know-who out of t-r-o-u-b-l-e." She spelled out the word so that Peter wouldn't understand.

The little boy stuffed his hands into his pockets and grinned as if he liked being the center of attention. "Wanna play ponopoly?" he asked hopefully.

"He means Monopoly," Stephanie explained to her friends. "But he really doesn't know how to play. He just stacks all the houses and hotels on the board, then crashes into them with his little metal car."

"PeeWee play ponopoly!" he insisted.

"No, Peter. Let's show them Fifi's tricks instead," Stephanie said.

Peter shook his head. "No."

"Oh, come on, Peter." Stephanie stood over him, her hands on her hips. "These are my friends, and they want to see what your dog can do."

Peter glared up at her. "No."

"Come on, PeeWee," Willie said coaxingly. "Don't you want to show us Fifi's tricks?"

"No, no, no, no, no!"

Stephanie took a deep breath. Then she gave Peter her brightest smile. "Wait a minute, Peter. Do you want to hear a secret?"

The little boy shrugged, then leaned up toward Stephanie.

She cupped her hands near his ear and whispered. Peter's lips curled into a smile.

"Okay," he said. He ran over to the poodle, picked her up, and carried her to the center of the room.

Missy counted five red bows on the tiny dog. She couldn't imagine Baby being comfortable with even one! It seemed that Fifi and Baby had very different personalities.

Peter lifted Fifi's front paws so that the poodle had to balance on her hind legs. "Walk up high, Fifi!" he instructed, letting go of her paws.

The dog tiptoed across the room like a little ballerina. Impressed, the girls clapped their hands.

"Good dog," Peter said, reaching into a box of doggie treats for Fifi's reward. After he patted the poodle on the head, he looked up at Stephanie. "Where's my penny?" he asked.

A sheepish expression crossed Stephanie's face as she opened her backpack and started digging inside. "I had to bribe him. A penny for each trick. Got any change?" she asked her friends.

The girls laughed and began searching their pockets for pennies.

"Here, PeeWee." Willie handed him a shiny copper penny.

"Pennies!" PeeWee ran to the coffee table and picked up his piggy bank. It was a molded plastic hog, blue with big orange polka dots. PeeWee dropped the coin into the bank and danced across the family room, singing, "Pennies, pennies, love those pennies!" He shook the piggy bank, making a loud rattling noise.

"Cut it out!" Stephanie groaned, putting her hands over her ears.

Missy waved a penny in the air. "How about another trick?" she asked, hoping the bribe would quiet down the three-year-old dynamo.

Peter led Fifi through her repertoire of tricks—batting a ball, rolling over, and playing dead. By the time the girls had run out of pennies, Missy was also sick of the racket Pee-Wee made every time he collected his fee. She was glad when the tricks were over and it was time to work on their Halloween costume.

With a stern warning to stay out of trouble *or else*, Peter was placed in front of the TV to watch his favorite cartoon show.

"My mom got us the yarn and the cardboard," Stephanie announced, dumping the contents of two shopping bags onto the floor.

The girls had planned to go trick-or-treating together and they'd designed a group costume —a gigantic plate of spaghetti and meatballs. Each person would be one-fourth of the plate. They would wear yarn for spaghetti, red felt for the tomato sauce, and a cardboard wedge for the plate. And each girl's head would be a big, juicy meatball.

"We should probably start with the plates," Stephanie said as she sorted through the supplies. "Let's make mine first, then you can use it as a pattern."

Wrapping a measuring tape around Stephanie's waist, Emily did some quick calculations. Then she drew an oval shape on the piece of cardboard.

Willie was in charge of cutting it out.

"Just keep her away from me when she has a pair of scissors in her hand," Stephanie said, raking her fingers through her hair. "She's dangerous."

With a bit of trimming, the cardboard fit neatly around Stephanie's waist. "How do I look?" Stephanie asked excitedly.

"Like an empty plate," Willie remarked as she cut into another piece of cardboard.

Stephanie ran upstairs to check out the costume in her bedroom mirror. Willie worked on the plates and Emily showed Missy how to loop and braid the yarn so that it looked like spaghetti.

"We can glue the ends to a cardboard band. When everything's done, we'll tape the band on like a necklace, and the pasta will hang down over our shoulders," Emily explained. Sewing was one of Emily's favorite hobbies, and she had come up with most of the ideas for the costume.

Missy smiled as she twisted a strand of yarn into a spaghetti braid. This was going to be the best Halloween of her life! All the costumes she'd worn in the past now seemed childish by comparison. A witch, a fairy princess, Raggedy Ann—even Wonder Woman seemed unoriginal compared to this year's idea.

"It's perfect!" Stephanie came prancing down the stairs and strutted into the room as if she were trying out for a beauty pageant.

Missy was beginning to wonder if the entire costume would be finished before Stephanie even lifted a finger to help.

"Let's see how the spaghetti looks." Emily held up the necklace with its dangling loops of yarn.

"Neat!" Stephanie fluffed the strands around her shoulders as if she were trying on a mink stole. "Now all I need is the sauce."

Emily shook out a sheet of red felt and wrapped it around Stephanie's shoulders. "We'll have to sew some loose stitches in the felt to gather it."

"Tomorrow," Willie said, putting down the scissors and stretching out on the floor. "Mr. Withers caught me throwing peas at Adam in the cafeteria. I've got to go home and write a composition about the importance of manners."

"I've got to go too," Missy said, checking her watch. "I have to take Baby for his afternoon walk."

"While you're at it," Stephanie told Missy, "maybe you can teach your dog some tricks. Can Baby walk on his hind legs like Fifi?"

Missy shook her head and laughed. "Baby would look pretty silly doing that." So what if Baby can't do special tricks? Missy thought as she turned to open the front door. He's still ten times better than that scrawny Fifi.

As Missy opened the door she saw something that made her burst out laughing.

"What's so funny?" Stephanie demanded.

Missy tried to answer, but the words kept getting tangled up with the bubbles of laughter in her throat. All she could do was point toward the front yard.

Suddenly curious, Stephanie, Emily, and Willie jumped to their feet and raced over to join Missy.

Peter and Fifi were playing tug of war with a batch of yarn. The entire skein had been unraveled throughout the yard, wrapped around shrubs, looped around tree branches, swirled around the lamppost.

"Hey!" Willie pointed out the door. "That's *our* yarn—our spaghetti!"

Stephanie threw open the door and charged out onto the front porch. "Oh, Peter," she shouted, her face turning red as a beet. "Stop acting like a three-year-old!"

Although Peter seemed confused at Stephanie's words, Fifi immediately took action. She let the yarn drop from her mouth and darted up the stairs toward Stephanie. Leaping up to stand on her hind legs, the poodle snapped and snarled at the yarn dangling from Stephanie's costume. "No, Fifi," Stephanie ordered. "Get down . . . get away . . . Mother!"

Willie couldn't help but watch as she backed down the block, making her way home. "Looks like Fifi's crazy about our costume," she called out.

Missy chuckled to herself as she crossed the street to her house. Maybe Fifi wasn't so bad after all.

CHAPTER

3

As Melissa opened the front door of her house, she was nearly knocked off her feet by the enormous furry whirlwind that came bounding toward her.

"Easy, Baby!" she said, scratching him behind the ears. Secretly she was pleased that her dog was so happy to see her.

"You're late," Mrs. Fremont called from the kitchen. "Baby's getting impatient for his walk."

"I was over at Stephanie's, working on our group Halloween costume," Missy explained as she reached for the dog's leash. "Ready to go, boy?" she asked the shaggy dog.

Baby thumped his tail excitedly as Missy strapped the leash onto his collar.

"Be back before dark, dear," Mrs. Fremont said as Baby led Missy out the door.

The park at the end of Sixty-fifth Street contained a grassy lawn with a narrow paved path for biking and roller-skating. The trees were an explosion of fall color now. Missy liked to gaze up at them, letting her eyes blur so that the red, yellow, and orange leaves blended together in a bright swirl of colors. Baby liked to sniff the piles of crispy brown leaves, though he looked funny afterward, when twigs and leaves clung to his fur.

As they walked along, Missy gave her dog the lowdown on Stephanie's guests. "Fifi's a little lady, all trimmed and clipped and dressed up with bows," she explained as Baby pulled at his leash in order to sniff around the trunk of a tree.

"But I wonder," Missy continued. "It seems as if Fifi's kind of stuck-up, just like Stephanie."

Baby cocked his head at her, playfully pushing at her knee with one paw. Missy sat on the soft grass beside him and smiled as she ruffled his fur. "I guess it's true, what they say about dogs resembling their owners. Everyone thinks we look alike, right, boy?"

Missy's curly red hair often tumbled over her eyes, just like Baby's soft gray fur. They were two of a kind, best friends, so Missy didn't mind being compared to the most lovable dog in the world.

A loud yapping noise made Baby's ears perk up.

"What's that?" Missy asked, looking across the path.

"Aruff, aruff, aruff!" Fifi was barking excitedly as she galloped through the park gates, followed closely by Peter, Stephanie, and Emily.

Baby jumped to his feet and stared nervously at the little dog.

"What's the matter, Baby?" Missy asked. "It's just Fifi, that poodle I told you about. Hey, you guys!" she called, waving to the girls.

Emily waved back. "Hi, Missy."

Stephanie crossed her arms and frowned as she looked at Missy and Baby. "I told you they'd be here!" she said to Emily in a loud, complaining voice.

Fifi continued to bark with excitement.

"Melissa Fremont, you'd better keep that big monster away from Fifi!" Stephanie shouted across the park.

"Baby's no monster! He's a friendly dog," Missy said. She tugged on Baby's leash, trying to get closer to the girls so that they could stop shouting at one another. But Baby whined and pulled back against his leash, making it hard for Missy to move him.

"I'm warning you," Stephanie said, wagging a finger at Missy. "If he even sneezes in Fifi's direction—you'll be sorry."

Finally, Missy had managed to drag Baby within a few feet of the others. "See?" Missy gasped, breathless from coaxing her heavy dog. "He's not going to hurt her."

Everyone watched in silence as the two dogs eyed each other. Fifi's tiny nose twitched, then she began to yap at Baby.

Missy tightened her grip on the leash, afraid that her dog would get mad at the little poodle.

But Baby didn't seem angry at all. With a whiny howl Baby crouched down like a coward.

"He looks like he's crying," Emily said.

"I can't believe it!" Stephanie laughed. She pointed at the big, whimpering dog. "Baby's afraid of Fifi. He's a wimpy chicken!"

"Wimpy!" said Peter in a positive voice as he stared at Baby.

"He is not," Missy insisted, tugging on Baby's leash. He whined again and rolled over on his back. She wasn't sure why her dog was acting so weird. She just wanted to get him away from the barking poodle. "Let's go," she said, pulling Baby away from the laughing girls. When they were a safe distance away, Baby dove into a pile of leaves and covered his eyes with his paws.

"It's okay, Baby." He whimpered when Missy patted him consolingly. "Stephanie should keep *her* dog on a leash!" The nerve of that girl! Calling Baby names when the real monster was that snapping poodle.

Baby just groaned and burrowed deeper into the pile of crisp leaves.

Missy cringed as laughter drifted through the park. She looked up in time to see Emily and Stephanie making strange gestures and giggling. "I can't believe they're making fun of you," Missy muttered. Then she groaned. "Oh, great. Now they're coming this way."

But Peter and Fifi headed over to the sand-box on the other side of the park. Missy was glad those two pests would be leaving the neighborhood in a few weeks.

Stephanie and Emily walked up to Missy and Baby.

"Oh, excuse us!" Stephanie said with a giggle. "We're looking for Baby, the chicken-hearted dog." Crouching low, she flapped her arms as if they were bird wings and cackled like a chicken. "Bock, bock!"

"Yeah," Emily added, joining her friend in a silly chicken imitation. "Chicken Fremont!"

"His name is Baby," Missy said, glaring at the girls. "And he's not a chicken. He's just not used to being barked at by spoiled poodles!"

But the girls were laughing so hard, they didn't hear Missy's words. They started to strut around and cackle like a pair of barnyard hens.

Missy scowled. Then she gave Baby's leash a gentle tug. "Let's go, Baby. Some people just don't know how to make their dogs behave."

Eagerly wagging his tail, Baby started toward the park gate. Missy was just about to leave the cackling hens without saying good-bye, when she saw Willie racing through the park toward them.

She ran up to Missy and Baby.

"I saw her! I saw her!" Willie was out of breath from running. "I saw her with my own eyes!"

"What are you talking about?" Missy asked.

Willie was pale and there was an excited expression on her face. Stephanie and Emily stopped acting like chickens and rushed over to her.

"What's going on?" demanded Stephanie.

"Who did you see?" asked Emily.

"Old Lady Rochester! I saw her myself," Willie exclaimed, still gasping for breath.

A cold chill traveled down Missy's spine, making her shiver. The sun was low in the sky, casting an eerie orange glow over everything.

"Now, calm down and tell us what happened," Stephanie insisted.

Willie nodded and took a deep breath. "Well, I went home to write my composition, but before I could even sharpen my pencil, my mom asked me to run over to Mrs. Owens's house and borrow a cup of milk for the casserole for—"

"Not that stuff!" Stephanie interrupted. "Tell us about Mrs. Rochester."

"I was getting to that," Willie said. "Anyway, when I walked by the house, Mrs. Rochester's ghost was standing in the upstairs window, staring down at me with big, bulging eyes. The ghost had wild curly red hair, just like Mrs. Rochester when she was young! And you know the rumor that the house is haunted by music? Well, the ghost was playing a flute! Old Mrs. Rochester used to play the flute night and day. She drove the neighbors crazy!"

"Wow," Emily murmured, her eyes wide with fear.

"You saw a real live ghost!" Stephanie exclaimed, giving Willie a shake. "You could be a hero!"

"Are you sure it was a ghost?" Missy asked timidly. "Maybe it was just the curtains moving or something."

"That's what I thought at first," Willie said, nodding. "But I could see her face so clearly. And when I heard that creepy music drifting down, I knew I wasn't imagining things."

"Maybe it's come back to catch unsuspecting trick-or-treaters on Halloween!" Stephanie said. "I'll bet that's it! Oh, Willie, you're so lucky it didn't get you. I'm never going by that house again," Stephanie vowed.

"Me either!" Emily added.

Missy was beginning to wonder who the real chicken was. "Aren't you guys going a little too far? I think there's probably some logical explanation—"

"Like what?" Stephanie snapped.

Missy tried to think of a good reason, but she couldn't come up with anything at the moment. "I don't know." She shrugged. "But I don't think it was really a ghost."

Willie shuddered. "Whatever it was, it was pretty spooky."

"You're pretty gutsy for a girl with a chicken dog," Stephanie sneered, wrinkling her nose at Baby. "Don't you believe in ghosts?"

Missy kneeled down next to Baby and brushed a few dried leaves off his fur. Did she believe in ghosts? She wasn't sure. She certainly didn't want to meet the ghosts of Three-Fingered Aggie or old Mrs. Rochester in the dark, musty corners of an attic. But they were just characters in stories. Like fairy-tale people . . . right?

"I—I'm not sure," Missy finally answered.

"Not sure?" Stephanie said. "I think you're bluffing. You're just a scaredy-cat, just like your dog."

"Baby's not a scaredy-cat!" Missy said. "And neither am I!"

Stephanie looked at her and a slow smile spread across her face. "Well, if you're so brave, why don't you go into the Rochester house on Halloween night? Better yet, you can spend the midnight hour inside the house. It's never locked, you know. We'll take you over there during my party and pick you up later—after the witching hour!"

"Oooh!" Emily squealed. "I would never do that! Anything could happen in a haunted house—on Halloween!"

"That's a dumb idea," Missy said. "I'll bet that house is cold . . . and there's probably no electricity either."

"So what?" Stephanie snapped. "You can take a blanket and a flashlight. And it'll be for just an hour."

"The midnight hour," Willie said in a spooky voice.

"And then everyone will know you're the bravest girl at Hills Point School," Emily said in a voice full of admiration.

"Or are you a chicken, just like your dog?" Stephanie asked. "You can take him with you. But after today, I don't think he'll give you much protection."

"Baby's a good watchdog," Missy insisted, starting to feel a sharp twinge in her stomach. All the girls were staring at her as if this were some kind of challenge. She wished Stephanie would just drop the whole idea of the haunted house.

Baby pushed his wet nose against her hand, urging her toward the park gate. Missy could tell that he wasn't crazy about Stephanie's plan either.

"We'll all be sleeping over at Stephanie's house, so your parents will never know," said Emily.

"And I'll show you where the house is—but I don't want to get too close," Willie added.

"So then it's settled." Stephanie crossed her arms and gave Missy a smug smile. "On Halloween night Missy has a late date—with a flute-playing ghost!"

CHAPTER 4

The idea of spending an hour in a haunted house on Halloween kept Missy tossing and turning all night long. As she munched on her corn flakes at breakfast, she decided to call off the whole stupid plan.

"It's ridiculous," she said to Baby.

He barked and thumped his tail against the kitchen floor. Obviously, he was in total agreement with Missy.

"What's ridiculous, dear?" Mrs. Fremont asked as she poured Missy a glass of juice.

"Oh . . . nothing, Mom." Missy thought about the story of Three-Fingered Aggie. She wondered if the poor girl who spent the night in the graveyard had a friend like Stephanie Cook.

But by the time she had a chance to talk to

Stephanie, it was too late. Everyone at the bus stop had heard about the dare even before Missy scrambled out the front door of her house.

At lunchtime the cafeteria was buzzing with stories about Missy and the haunted house. Everyone seemed to think she was a hero already. If she backed out now, every kid at Hills Point School would laugh at Melissa Fremont and her chicken-hearted dog.

"You're so brave," Emily told her.

At the moment Missy didn't feel brave at all. She barely had the courage to eat the Thursday lunch special, Tex-Mex chili.

Stephanie sat down next to Missy. She'd brought her lunch in a pretty pastel-colored paper bag. "Yuck!" she said, staring down at Missy's chili. "I'm glad I don't have to eat that goop." Stephanie's lunch included tiny sandwich squares with the crusts removed, and thinly sliced carrot sticks.

"Everyone's talking about the haunted house," Stephanie said proudly. "*Now* do you believe in ghosts?"

Missy dropped her spoon in her chili. "I never said I didn't. I just think some people let their imagination get the best of them."

"Oh, really?" Stephanie smoothed back her blond hair. "And how about your chicken-hearted dog? I think Fifi misses him. She needs something to chase."

Missy's mouth tightened. "Baby is a brave

dog. In fact, he's looking forward to a night out."

Stephanie just smiled.

"Are you sure you want to go through with this?" Willie asked a few minutes later while Stephanie was standing in the milk line. "Stephanie is just shooting off her mouth. If you back out, everything will die down in a few days."

"And you've never even *seen* the Rochester house," Emily added. "That place looks spooky even in the daytime."

Missy shook her head. "Nope, we're going to do it," she told the girls. "Even if the house is creepy-looking, we'll stay. Stephanie is just trying to scare me."

Willie laughed nervously. "I'd rather be safe than scared to death," she said.

Missy shivered at her words. She didn't really believe in haunted houses or ghosts . . . but why was she taking this stupid dare?

Three-Fingered Aggie's warning seemed to pop into her head. *Dare not, die not!* If she and Baby stayed in the Rochester house, would they be flirting with the spirits from the great beyond?

On Friday afternoon Missy was standing in the bus line in front of the school, when her classmate Ashley Woods approached her.

"Are you a good witch or a bad witch?" Ashley asked curiously.

Missy laughed as she recognized one of the lines from the movie *The Wizard of Oz.* "I'm not a witch at all!" she said, answering Ashley with the next line from the movie.

"Oh, really?" Ashley narrowed her small, beady eyes suspiciously. "I've heard the rumors about you and your dog. How are you going to lift the evil spell on the old Rochester house? Will you use a magic wand or a special saying?" Ashley moved closer and squeezed Missy's arm. "Listen," she whispered as if she were telling a secret. "Do you have a spell I could use on my jerky little brother?"

"No!" Missy squealed. Sometimes she couldn't believe what a nerd Ashley was. "None of that stuff is true. I'm not a witch and I don't know any magic spells. Who told you that?"

"Stephanie Cook," Ashley said. "Does that mean you're *not* spending Halloween night in the old Rochester house?"

"Well, that part is true," said Missy. She stared at the ground, trying to ignore the sharp twinge that twisted her stomach every time someone mentioned Halloween.

Ashley hugged her books to her chest. "Then you must be a witch. No one would be dumb enough to spend Halloween night in a haunted house unless they had some magical powers."

No one except dumb old me, Missy thought with a frown. She looked up, relieved to see the school bus pulling up at the curb.

"I'm surprised that you still ride the bus," Ashley said. "If I were a witch, I'd just fly."

Missy shook her head. Things were really getting out of hand. Soon people would start believing that she brewed magic potions down in her basement! " 'Bye, Ashley," Missy said.

Ashley waved. "Don't worry. I won't tell anyone else about your magical powers," she said loudly as Missy climbed aboard the bus.

If I had magical power, Missy thought as she sat down beside Emily, I would turn Stephanie Cook into a frog!

That night Missy dreamed she was surrounded by clouds of fluffy pink cotton candy. She floated through the air, occasionally reaching out to take a bite of the soft sweet puffs. Then she felt something cool and moist press against her face and woke up.

Baby had crawled into bed with her. Now he was nudging her with his nose. The cotton candy puffs had been tufts of Baby's soft fur.

The memory of her dream left a smile on Missy's face. But as her sweet dream faded away, Missy realized that it was Saturday morning—Halloween. She rolled over and hugged her pillow, wondering if she'd ever make it back to her safe, cozy bed.

"Tonight's the night," she told Baby. "Are you scared?"

He licked her hand and wagged his tail.

"You're not?" Missy asked. "That's good. Maybe I am becoming a scaredy-cat. It's only an hour, right, boy?"

Baby barked in agreement.

Missy wondered what the haunted house would be like. Maybe she wouldn't be so frightened if she knew how the Rochester place looked. "I've got an idea. Maybe we should investigate the haunted house on our own. By the light of day, of course." Baby jumped off the bed and went to Missy's bedroom door. Reaching up with a paw, he pulled Missy's robe from its hook. Then he gripped the robe between his teeth and dragged it over to Missy.

Missy laughed. "You're really eager to start the day. I forgot how much you liked Halloween and trick-or-treating." She slipped on the robe and stretched.

Halloween used to be one of Missy's favorite days too. But Stephanie's dare had ruined her fun in the last few days. Even last night, when the girls finished their costume, Missy was too tense to enjoy the excitement.

Baby pushed open the bedroom door and barked. The aroma of sugar and cinnamon filled the air.

"French toast!" exclaimed Missy. So that was why Baby was so excited. Missy and Baby both loved French toast.

Missy patted Baby's head. "Mom sure knows how to cheer us up!" She and Baby raced down the stairs, eager to gobble down a delicious breakfast.

The front of the Rochester house looked like the face of a giant, sleeping monster.

Afraid to get too close, Missy stood across the street from the huge old place.

"It does look spooky," she whispered.

Baby barked at the house, then shuffled back and forth in front of Missy. Although he'd been afraid of Fifi, Baby didn't seem bothered by the haunted house.

"This is close enough," Missy told him. "We don't have to go inside until later."

Missy sat down on the curb to study the old mansion. She had been on Willie's block before, but had never noticed the abandoned house with its yard full of ugly weeds.

As Missy stared at the house a chill ran down her spine. She felt as though someone were staring back at her. Was the house checking *her* out too?

The arched double doors looked like a grim, frowning mouth. All the windows were covered with boards except for the two on the top floor. They were round and black, like two beady eyes. The gabled roof had two pointed peaks, which made Missy think of a monster's horns.

"Maybe it just needs some fixing up," Missy suggested. If she kept studying the house, maybe she could come up with the courage to face it alone after dark.

Large sycamore trees hung over the walk. "Maybe if someone trimmed those hedges and those big, black trees . . ."

Baby barked and shook his head.

"You're right," she admitted. She scratched him behind the ears. "It does look kind of hopeless."

On the rest of the block, kids were out playing, riding bikes, and tossing balls. There were even a few grownups raking leaves.

But there was no sign of life near the Rochester house. It seemed as if a dark cloud of doom hung over the place.

"Come on," Missy said to Baby. "Let's get a closer look."

Carefully they crossed the street and walked toward the house. Missy had to force her feet to move forward.

She reached the edge of the yard and stopped. The bushes on the side of the house seemed to be moving.

"Wait a minute," she said to Baby, who was eager to go on. She watched.

One of the bushes swayed, and then a figure appeared. Missy felt her heart leap into her throat. Someone was there!

She grabbed hold of Baby's leash and cautiously crept forward.

Suddenly the figure moved away from the hedge. Missy almost screamed in terror, until she recognized Stephanie Cook.

"Hey," Missy called, releasing Baby's leash and running toward her friend.

"Ahh!" Stephanie screamed. She clutched at her throat, dropping something.

When she realized it was just Missy and her

dog, Stephanie took a deep breath and marched forward. "You shouldn't sneak up on people like that. What are you doing here anyway?" she asked, moving away from the hedges toward Missy and Baby.

"We thought we'd come over and see where we'll be spending the midnight hour," Missy said, trying her best to sound cheerful. She looked up at the house and saw the peeling paint and one shutter dangling from a hinge. "It's sort of . . . rundown-looking."

"What did you expect from a haunted house?" smirked Stephanie. "Red carpets and a doorman?"

Missy shrugged. "What are you doing here?" she asked.

Stephanie looked away. "Oh . . . nothing."

"Nothing?" Missy found that hard to believe. She was sure that Stephanie Cook did not usually spend Saturdays lurking in shrubs. Especially at haunted houses.

"Nothing," Stephanie repeated. "Really. I just wanted to make sure that the house was ready for tonight. You know. I was afraid that someone had moved in or something."

Baby barked, making Stephanie flinch.

Missy also doubted Stephanie's excuse.

"Actually," Stephanie continued, "I was just leaving. I've got to get home and set things up for the party tonight."

Baby started barking again, then ran toward the front of the house.

"Baby, wait!" Missy cried, racing after him.

When she caught up with him, he was panting and barking at something inside the house. Missy looked up. "What's wrong, boy?"

Just then a figure appeared in one of the upstairs windows. Baby barked again.

Missy couldn't believe her eyes. "Look!" she shouted, pointing up at the window.

"Aaahh!" Stephanie screeched. "It's Mrs. Rochester!"

Missy's heart thundered in her chest like a wild drum roll. For one breathless moment she stared at the window, trying to make out the person looking down at them.

"Run!" Stephanie screamed. "Run for your life!"

The two girls fled down the street, with Baby following closely behind them.

Stephanie nearly tripped over a little boy riding a tricycle, but she didn't slow down.

Missy made herself run fast and hard. Even when her lungs began to burn, she forced herself to keep going.

The thought of the figure in the window made her run even faster. That was no shifting curtain, and she knew it wasn't a reflection.

She had seen a woman with wild, flowing red hair and huge, bulging eyes.

Melissa Fremont had seen the ghost of Mrs. Rochester!

CHAPTER

5

"Something wrong with your veal scaloppini?" Mrs. Fremont asked.

Missy had been sitting at the table for almost half an hour, but she'd eaten only a few bites of her dinner. "No, it's fine," she said, forcing herself to smile.

"You're going to lose your membership in the clean plate club," Mr. Fremont teased her.

"I'm too old for that stuff now, Dad," Missy said. She cut off another bite of meat and pushed it across her plate.

"Honey, if you're not going to eat it, please don't mutilate it." Missy's mom frowned. "Are you feeling okay, dear? Suddenly you look as though you just saw a ghost."

"You do look a little pale," Mr. Fremont added.

Missy shook her head. "I'm fine," she said quickly. "I'm just not very hungry." She stared down at her plate.

"That's not a good sign," said Mrs. Fremont. "Are you sure you want to go to this sleep-over tonight, Missy?"

Missy's head bolted up. "I have to go! I have to! Please, Mom."

"All right, all right," Mrs. Fremont said. She reached over and felt Missy's forehead. "A little warm, but not feverish." She shrugged, then picked up her fork again.

"Just fright-night nerves," Mr. Fremont said, smiling.

Missy swallowed a piece of veal and asked, "What's that?"

"Oh, you know . . . Halloween night. All the ghosts and hobgoblins wandering around. Not a fit night for man or beast . . ."

The piece of meat suddenly seemed to be stuck in Missy's throat. "Really?" she croaked. "Do you believe in ghosts, Dad?"

"Oh . . . sure!" he answered.

Missy dropped her fork. "You do?"

Mr. Fremont nodded. "And all those things that go bump in the night."

Missy's mother helped herself to another spoonful of rice. "William, I think you're scaring her," she said to Missy's father. "I *know* you're scaring me."

Mr. Fremont smiled at his daughter. "Is that the problem? Are you suffering from a case of the Halloween jitters?"

"Yes." Missy nodded. "I mean, I guess so. Do you think a ghost would hurt a kid my age?" she asked earnestly.

"I don't like the sound of this conversation," Mrs. Fremont said. "What made you so concerned about ghosts, Missy?"

"Just curious," she answered. She chased a mushroom around her plate. "The kids at school say that the old Rochester house is haunted."

Missy's dad laughed. "Is that so?"

Missy nodded, her eyes wide with fear. "And some of the kids ... well, some people have seen the ghost of Mrs. Rochester inside the house."

Mr. Fremont began to laugh so hard that tears formed in his eyes.

"What's so funny?" Missy asked him.

"The ... the ghost of Mrs. Rochester?" he repeated, still chuckling.

"Your father and I have met Mrs. Rochester's great-niece, and she's a lovely woman," Missy's mom explained. "Isn't it funny how rumors get started?"

Missy chewed on a slice of veal and wondered about her father and mother. She knew they would miss her if ... if she went into the Rochester house ... and didn't get out alive.

"But don't let Halloween scare you," said Missy's dad. "You have nothing to fear but fear itself."

"What about you, Mom?" Missy asked. "Do you believe in ghosts?"

Mrs. Fremont nodded. "Friendly ghosts, dear," she answered. "Like Casper and his buddies."

"What a delicious-looking meatball!" Mr. Fremont raved.

Missy twirled through the living room, modeling her Halloween costume. "And I'm only one fourth of the plate," she reminded him. She loved the idea of their group costume. If only she didn't have the black cloud of the haunted house hanging over her . . . then she could just have fun.

"It certainly was an original idea," Missy's mother agreed. "I'll bet you girls will be the only plate of spaghetti and meatballs in Indianapolis."

Baby shook his back end and barked.

"Ready to go?" Missy asked him.

He barked again and nudged her sleeping bag with his nose.

Missy stood hesitantly at the front door. After making sure her flashlight was tucked inside her overnight case, she turned to her parents.

"I just want you both to know," she said with a lump in her throat, "that no matter what happens, you've always been the best parents in the whole wide world!"

Mr. and Mrs. Fremont looked at each other curiously.

"And we love you too, Missy," Mr. Fremont said.

"But Missy," Mrs. Fremont said, "we're going to see you again in ten minutes, when you and the girls stop by for trick-or-treat goodies."

"Oh, yeah." Missy shrugged. "In that case, I'll see you later."

Missy and Baby walked up the steps to Stephanie's house. Missy rang the bell.

"It's another meatball-head!" Denise announced as she opened the door.

Missy smiled at Stephanie's little sister. Denise was dressed as a fairy princess, with a glittering cape and crown.

"You may enter," Denise ordered with a wave of her wand. "But keep Baby outside, or Fifi will go crazy."

Missy had almost forgotten about the nasty poodle that had gotten Baby into so much trouble. Out on the front porch, she explained the situation to her dog. "It'll be for just a few minutes, then you can go trick-or-treating with us." She tied Baby's leash to the porch railing.

Baby thumped his tail against the porch, then sat down to wait.

Back inside, everyone was excited about the spaghetti-and-meatball costume.

"How adorable!" Mrs. Cook exclaimed, looking at the girls.

"Good. Now that Missy's finally here, we can take a group picture," Stephanie said. In her usual bossy manner she began to move everyone into position for the photo. Willie, who was the tallest, stood in the center.

"The noodles look neat," Missy told Emily. "You did a great job designing them."

Emily smiled. "Thanks, Missy."

"Stop talking, you two, and look at the camera!" Stephanie ordered.

"Okay, girls." Mrs. Cook focused the camera. "Everyone smile and say spaghetti with cheese."

"Cheese!" the girls shouted.

Mrs. Cook snapped the picture.

"Cheese!" shouted Peter as he came bounding down the stairs. Fifi was behind him, yapping away. Peter was wearing several sheets of gray construction paper that had been stapled together. He danced around the family room in a funny-looking costume. "PeeWee's the cheese! PeeWee's the cheese!"

"What's that he's wearing?" Willie asked.

"He *thinks* he's a jar of grated cheese," Stephanie answered. "And he *thinks* he's going trick-or-treating with us."

Willie wrinkled her nose. "Good grief!"

"Well, he's not going with me!" Denise insisted. "Fairies are never seen with jars of cheese!"

"Please don't argue, girls," Stephanie's mother said. "Peter will go with the older girls, Denise."

"But, Mom—" Stephanie whined.

"And that's final." Mrs. Cook leaned down to pull Peter's cap over his ears. "You will be a good boy, won't you?"

He nodded.

Stephanie gave everyone a paper sack with a pumpkin printed on it. "Okay, let's go."

The girls filed out the front door. Stephanie waited for Peter, but blocked the door when Fifi tried to sneak out.

"You're staying home," she said to the little dog. "You bark too much."

The poodle barked again and glared at Baby.

"Let's get out of here before Fifi scares your dog again," Stephanie told Missy.

The street was crowded with groups of kids in costumes. Since Missy's house was right across the street, they stopped there first.

"Trick-or-treat!" the girls cried.

"Oh, William, I do believe our dinner's arrived!" Mrs. Fremont remarked.

The girls laughed and opened their bags.

"A delicious costume," Missy's dad said as he tossed a candy bar into each bag.

"PeeWee's the cheese!" Peter shouted, jumping up and down.

"I can see that," Mrs. Fremont said as she handed the little boy a candy bar.

Willie nudged Stephanie and asked, "Is he going to do that at every house?"

"He's only three," Stephanie snapped. "He can't help it."

But Missy didn't think his age was any excuse for bad manners.

Peter did the same little dance for Mrs. Green. When the girls went to Willie's house, he asked Mrs. Wagnalls for two treats.

"Isn't he just the cutest thing," said Mrs. Wagnalls.

"What a pest," Willie muttered.

Mrs. Wagnalls also made a fuss over Baby. She gave him a big hug, and a candy bar of his own, which pleased Missy.

The spaghetti-and-meatball costume was a big hit. Everyone liked the fancy yarn noodles and cardboard plates.

But all too soon the girls had finished trick-or-treating. They'd been to see everyone they knew in each of their neighborhoods, and it was time to go back to Stephanie's house.

The sharp pain in Missy's stomach was beginning to get worse. Soon it would be time to enter the haunted house. Suddenly Missy wished she did have a magic wand and a magic spell or two. Even a fake prop or some magic words would be better than facing the ghost of old Mrs. Rochester empty-handed.

Sprawled on the floor of Stephanie's family room, the girls sorted out their treats. There was a creature feature on television, but Missy tried not to watch. Vampires and werewolves were the last thing she needed to see right now.

The clock raced on.

Missy unwrapped one of her favorite candies, a cherry-chew, and popped it into her mouth. If this was her last treat, she wanted to enjoy it.

"Eleven-thirty," Stephanie announced. "We'd better get going."

Missy nearly swallowed the candy whole. Silently she picked up her flashlight and sleeping bag and went out the door.

The wind had picked up and the leaves on the trees rustled as the girls walked toward the Rochester house.

"Do you think it's going to rain?" Emily asked, watching the clouds sweep past the yellow moon.

"Shhh, we're getting close," Stephanie said as they turned the last corner. "We don't want to wake up Mrs. Rochester's ghost while *we're* nearby."

Emily shuddered. "Don't say stuff like that!"

"Quiet!" Stephanie poked her, and Emily covered her mouth.

The Rochester house stood before them like a towering black mountain outlined against the night sky.

Stephanie led the girls up to the front entrance, then stopped. "This is far enough for us."

"Wow," Emily gasped, blinking at the dark, looming house. "Are you sure you want to go through with this, Missy?"

"We're sure," Missy said. She unhooked Baby's leash and tied it around her waist.

Baby barked and galloped up the front steps.

As Missy followed Baby, the splintered wooden steps creaked under her feet.

The front porch sagged in the middle, and some of the rails were broken. When she reached the huge double doors, Missy paused and looked back at her friends. The twisted sycamore trees towered over the walk, blocking out the moonlight. The trees' branches seemed to be reaching out to her, like giant fingers.

"Go on," Stephanie ordered. "Open the door."

Missy drew in a breath and twisted the knob. She pulled at the door, but it wouldn't budge. "It's locked," she called back, secretly relieved.

"It can't be," Stephanie snapped. She gave Willie a shove. "Go help her."

With a grim frown Willie crept onto the porch and tried the door. "She's right," she said, lifting a foot against the frame to get a better grip. "This door's sealed up tight."

"What do you mean, it's locked?" Stephanie stamped her foot in anger. "It was open when I—I mean, it's always open."

Willie shrugged. "But it's locked now. I guess the dare is off."

"No way!" Stephanie said huffily, stomping up the rickety steps. "These two aren't getting off so easily. They're going inside—even if I have to open the door with my teeth!"

Under Stephanie's orders the girls pulled and shoved and kicked at the door. Emily found an old plank from the porch rail and wedged it into the crack under the door.

The girls pulled with all their might. Finally the rusty knob moved and the door popped open with a loud bang.

The girls ended up sprawled on the porch, staring at the black hole of darkness inside.

"After all this trouble, you'd better not back out now," Stephanie muttered. She stood up and rubbed the seat of her pants.

"We won't," Missy said quietly. Her heart was pounding as she rose and rubbed her sweaty hands on her jeans.

"Good luck, Missy," Emily said.

Missy stood in the doorway with Baby at her side. "And you'll be back in an hour?" she asked.

"Sure," Willie promised. "We'll meet you right here—at one o'clock sharp."

"*If* there's anything left of you," Stephanie added.

"Good-bye," Missy called to her friends. She hoped this didn't mean good-bye forever.

With her hand on Baby's head, she took a deep breath and stepped into the pitch-black darkness.

CHAPTER

6

"**I** don't believe in ghosts. I don't believe in ghosts," Missy whispered over and over again. Cautiously, she crept forward, staying close to her shaggy dog.

"Let's stick close together, Baby."

He barked, then nudged her hand.

"Oh, right," Missy said, looking down at the flashlight clenched in her fist. She turned it on and pointed the beam in front of her.

A huge wooden staircase rose before her. The fancy carved railings were covered with cobwebs.

"We're *not* going upstairs," she said, moving the beam to her right.

A wide hallway led to two closed doors. And right beside Missy was an arched doorway, framing an open parlor.

"Let's try this room," Missy said. "It's close to the door." She reached down to take Baby's collar. If Baby stayed by her side, she wouldn't be quite so scared.

When Missy peered inside the room, her heart jumped into her throat. "Ghosts!" she gasped.

The parlor was filled with bulky white figures.

Missy moved the light beam over them, staring in frightened silence. They didn't move. A moment later, she realized that her "ghosts" were just chairs covered with white sheets.

With a sigh of relief Missy let go of Baby's collar. She shone the flashlight around the rest of the room. The walls were lined with bookcases that stretched from the dusty floor to the high ceiling. In the center of one wall there was a brick fireplace with a portrait hanging over it.

"This must have been Mrs. Rochester's library," Missy told Baby. As she tiptoed through the doorway, a sticky cobweb brushed her cheek. "Yuck!" she gasped, quickly brushing it away.

Baby sniffed around the room, checking things out for himself.

Missy walked over to the fireplace.

"Look, Baby," Missy said, pointing to the painting. "That must be Mrs. Rochester."

Sure enough, the woman in the painting had long red hair and was holding a flute.

"Now, *she* doesn't look spooky." The woman's kindly smile reminded Missy of her mom. Somehow, it boosted her courage a little.

There were two tall candles and a box of matches on top of the mantel. Missy lit them, hoping to brighten up the room.

"That's much cozier," she said to Baby. But Baby was busy scratching at one of the lower book shelves.

Missy went over to see what he was looking at. When she pulled the leather-bound book from its spot, a large, hairy spider jumped out.

"Aaah!" she screamed, dropping the book.

Baby growled and chased the spider until it disappeared beneath the edge of the rug.

"Oh, Baby," Missy said, giving him a big hug. "It was just a spider. I'm such a scaredy-cat, and you're the bravest dog in the world!"

Baby licked Missy on the cheek, then hopped onto a sofa that was covered with a white sheet.

Missy picked up the book she had dropped and sat down next to her dog.

"That's a good idea. Maybe we should just relax. I'll read to you. And before we know it, the . . . the midnight hour will be over, and the girls will be back to pick us up."

A strange creaking noise whined overhead.

"What's that?" Missy moved closer to Baby.

But Baby didn't seem alarmed. His ears were flat against his head.

Missy gritted her teeth when she heard the creaking noise again. It sounded like footsteps upstairs.

Baby just yawned and nudged the book with his nose.

"You're right," Missy told him. "I'm being silly. I don't believe in ghosts." She dusted off the book and looked at the title.

"It's called *Treasure Island*. You might like this one, Baby. It's all about pirates, I think."

Snuggled next to her dog on the sofa, Missy began to read out loud. She stopped every time she heard the creaking noise.

"What do you think that is?" she asked Baby. "Mice? Or maybe bats?" She shivered. Haunted houses could be filled with all kinds of strange creatures.

Baby hopped off the sofa and started sniffing around the bookcase again. He barked twice, trying to get Missy's attention.

"Did you find another book to read?" Missy asked, kneeling beside him. She hoped there wasn't another spider too.

Baby kept scratching at a fat red book on one of the lower shelves.

When Missy tried to pull it out, it wouldn't budge. "This must be a very heavy book," she said.

With all her might Missy pulled again. The red book slid out with a grinding noise—and the entire bookcase beside it popped open!

"Oh my gosh!" Missy gasped. There was a hole in the wall behind the bookcase.

Baby stepped into the opening and barked.

Missy followed him. It was dark inside, but she used her flashlight to light the way.

"It's a hidden passage!" she exclaimed.

A narrow staircase twisted upward. Even with her flashlight Missy couldn't see how far it went. Baby climbed the bottom steps, eager to go on.

"No, Baby." Missy shook her head. "It's not safe." Cautiously she backed out of the opening. "Come on, Baby," she called.

He followed her out but stayed near the bookcase, sniffing curiously.

"A secret passageway," Missy said to herself. She thought it was an exciting discovery. "I wonder if Mrs. Rochester knew it was there?"

Just then some music started to drift through the house. It began softly, then grew stronger and louder as the melody changed. Missy's heart thudded in her chest. Her palms were beginning to sweat again.

She knew that sound. Someone was playing a flute.

"Oh, no!" Missy clapped her hands over her ears. "I don't believe in ghosts! I don't, I don't, I don't!"

Baby lifted his head to the ceiling and began to howl.

Missy was surprised. Since her father played the viola and her mother played the piano, Baby was used to hearing music. Why was he howling now?

"Baby, sshhh!" Missy whispered. "They'll hear you."

But Baby kept howling away.

As the music seemed to move overhead, Baby followed it.

"Please, Baby," Missy said. She didn't like the haunted music, either, but she didn't want to offend Mrs. Rochester's ghost.

Suddenly the music got much louder. Baby followed the sound to the hidden staircase.

"Baby, come back!" Missy begged.

But he stepped into the opening and howled up the stairs.

Missy leaned into the dark opening and reached for her dog's collar. But her hands slipped along his fluffy fur. He was too far ahead of her.

Baby's ears perked up. He was ready for a chase. With an excited bark he bounded up the stairs and disappeared into the darkness.

"Baby!" Missy cried. "Come back!"

CHAPTER 7

"**B**aby, where are you going?"

Missy ran up the first few steps, then paused. She moved the flashlight beam across the dark staircase, but Baby was nowhere in sight.

How could he run off like this?

The flute music continued as Missy peered up the stairs. Should she go up?

She had to find her dog, but she felt frozen in place. "I can't do it," she whispered. She felt cold and scared. Her knees had begun to shake beneath her.

"I guess I'm the big chicken after all." She returned to the room and began to pace in front of the brick fireplace.

"Don't panic," she told herself. Still feeling chilled, she pulled the sheet off the couch and wrapped it around her shoulders.

You have nothing to fear but fear itself. Her father's words echoed through her mind. She couldn't let this creepy house get to her. There had to be a logical explanation for the flute music.

Maybe it was wind blowing through the pipes. As the music continued, Missy knew that couldn't be true. The melody was pretty, like a sad song. The wind wouldn't sound like a symphony piece.

Maybe it was a recording, a tape that had been set up by . . . by Stephanie! Maybe that was why she had been snooping around the haunted house earlier that day.

Missy paced back and forth, wondering what to do. She had to get her dog back and get out of this spooky place. She would deal with Miss Stephanie Cook later.

Suddenly the flute music stopped.

Missy had gotten so used to it that the silence seemed eerie. Then she heard the patter of footsteps growing louder . . . and louder.

When she heard Baby's happy bark, she nearly fainted with relief. A moment later he came trotting down the hidden staircase.

"Oh, Baby!" She threw her arms around him and gave him a giant hug. "Am I glad to see you! Let's get out of here. I don't care what anyone thinks. I have a feeling this is all one of Stephanie's dirty tricks!"

Baby barked and wagged his tail.

"You're not a chicken, and neither am I!

We're two of the bravest . . . best . . ." Missy stopped. There was something hanging around Baby's furry neck.

"What's this?" she asked. She touched the soft necklace. It was a chain of fresh daisies. "This is beautiful. Where did you find it?"

Baby barked and nodded toward the stairs.

A chain of daisies.

A little alarm went off in Missy's brain. "Wasn't there something about a daisy necklace in the legend of Three-Fingered Aggie?" she asked her dog.

Baby wagged his tail.

"There was," Missy said. "The girl in the graveyard . . . when they found her, she was wearing a chain of daisies." Missy's palms were beginning to sweat again. "Oh, Baby, we've got to get out of this house!"

Quickly Missy picked up her sleeping bag, tucked it under her arm, and grabbed Baby by the collar. "Let's go!"

They scrambled out of the parlor and raced toward the front door.

Missy grabbed the doorknob and turned, but nothing happened. "Oh, it's stuck again!"

She pushed and shoved against the tall wooden door, but it wouldn't open. "I can't believe this!" she said, pounding the door with her fist.

Baby barked and started to nudge her away from the door.

Missy pointed the flashlight toward the other

end of the hall. "You're right," she told Baby. "Maybe we should try the back door."

Together she and Baby ran down the hall toward two closed doors.

"This one better not be stuck," Missy said as she gripped the doorknob.

The knob turned and the door opened easily. Missy let out a scream when she saw what was hanging on the other side. A skeleton, white and bony, dangled in the doorway.

"Ahhh!" she yelped, jumping back and stumbling over Baby. Together they landed in a heap on the floor.

At that moment the lilting music started again. "Oh, no," Missy groaned.

Baby sat up, pricked his ears, and started howling.

"Not again." Missy stood up and brushed her jeans off. She frowned at the hanging skeleton, then quickly turned away. She didn't want to try the second door. Who knew what was hanging behind it? And at the end of the hallway was a black wall. "How are we going to get out of here, Baby?"

There was no way out. What were they going to do?

Baby howled again, then scampered toward the main staircase.

"Wait!" Missy shouted. She was running out of courage and strength. Hot tears burned the back of her eyes as she chased after her dog.

He was halfway up the stairs when she reached him.

"Where are you going? Is there a way out from up there?" she asked.

Out of breath and teary-eyed, Missy flashed the beam of light up the stairs.

Suddenly she saw writing on the wall at the top of the stairs. She walked up the stairs. It was a message, scrawled in black crayon:

DARE NOT, DIE NOT!

Missy couldn't believe her eyes. "Three-Fingered Aggie!" she whispered over the lump that was forming in her throat.

But it was just a ghost story, wasn't it? Missy wasn't quite so sure anymore.

Missy collapsed on the top step and leaned against the wall.

Baby sat next to her and licked her hand. She knew he was trying to make her feel better, but she couldn't stop her tears.

What was Three-Fingered Aggie doing in Mrs. Rochester's house, Missy wondered. Did ghosts haunt houses in groups?

She knew that Stephanie could have left the message on the wall, but what about the chain of daisies around Baby's neck?

And if Stephanie was planning all these tricks, who was standing at the window earlier that day? Missy sniffed back a tear.

There had to be a logical explanation for all these odd events. There just had to be.

"I don't believe in Three-Fingered Aggie. I don't believe in ghosts," she whispered, squeezing her eyes shut.

The flute music stopped, and she breathed a sigh of relief.

"I don't believe in ghosts. I don't—" She opened her eyes and gasped.

Someone dressed in white was standing at the end of the second-story hallway, holding a golden candle.

Missy rubbed the tears from her eyes, but the figure in white didn't go way. Instead, it started walking toward her.

Missy gulped. "I'm sorry," she called out to the ghost. It had wild, flowing red hair, just like the woman in the portrait downstairs.

Baby barked at the figure with the candle.

"We're both sorry," Missy pleaded. "We . . . we promise we'll never ever bother your haunted house again!" Her voice sounded squeaky.

But the ghost kept coming closer . . . and closer.

Missy covered her face with her hands and whispered, "I do believe in ghosts . . . I do, I do, I do!"

CHAPTER

8

"**M**issy?" the ghost called out to her.

The ghost even knew her name! Missy leaned against her shaggy dog. She was too afraid to open her eyes.

"Missy?" the ghost spoke again.

It wasn't a creepy voice, Missy realized. Actually, it seemed nice. Maybe this is a friendly ghost, Missy thought as she opened one eye.

"I'm sorry if I scared you too much." The ghost sighed. "Well, honestly, I meant to frighten you and your friends—just a little. But I didn't mean to make you cry."

Missy eyed the figure cautiously. In the golden light of the candle the ghost didn't look like a ghost at all. In fact, she looked like a woman in a silky white gown. Her eyes weren't bulging anymore, and she was smiling.

Baby trotted over to the figure in white and licked her hand.

"Baby, no!" Missy said, grabbing at her dog. "Don't touch that ghost!"

The woman laughed. "Is that what you think? That I'm the ghost of old Mrs. Rochester?"

The lump in Missy's throat made it hard for her to speak. "I thought so," she gulped. "But now I'm not so sure."

The figure in white patted Baby on the head, then sat on the step next to Missy. "Well, I'm a flesh-and-blood woman. I guess you don't remember me. I play in the Indianapolis Symphony with your father. I visited your house last week while you were having a party."

Missy stared at the woman. "I do remember you now."

The woman smiled at Missy. "My name is Melody Rochester Smith." She held out her hand to Missy.

Stunned, Missy shook the woman's hand. "You're related to old Mrs. Rochester?"

Melody nodded. "She was my great-aunt. When I heard that the Indianapolis Symphony needed someone to play the flute, I decided to move here and fix up Aunt Melody's house. My husband's an architect, and he's very excited about this place. He'll be joining me here as soon as he closes up our apartment in Chicago."

With a sigh of relief Missy wiped the last of the tears from her eyes. Finally things were

beginning to make sense. "So you've been living here all along?" Missy asked.

Melody nodded. "Only on the top floor. The rest of this house needs a lot of work—and a good cleaning," she said, brushing a speck of dust from her white gown. "Now, you tell me, young lady, what you and this big adorable dog are doing in my house."

"We're really sorry," Missy said. She told Melody all about Stephanie's dare. She described how Fifi had frightened Baby in the park, and how Stephanie had spread the story of the haunted house to everyone at school. "If Baby and I didn't go through with Stephanie's plan, all the kids at Hills Point would have called us chickens."

Baby barked in agreement.

"I see," Melody said. "So Stephanie is the blond girl who was snooping around here earlier this morning?"

Missy nodded.

"She's the one I was trying to scare," Melody admitted. "I overheard your ghost stories about Three-Fingered Aggie and Aunt Melody. It started out as a joke. I stood in the upstairs window and played my flute wearing these." She pulled a pair of ugly plastic eyeballs from the pocket of her robe.

Missy laughed at the funny disguise.

Melody continued. "When I saw Stephanie hanging a skeleton in my kitchen doorway, I knew something odd was going on. That's when

I took things a step further. I made the daisy chain and wrote Three-Fingered Aggie's message on the wall."

Missy touched the daisies that hung around Baby's thick neck. "I can understand a joke. But why did you want to scare us?" she asked.

Melody sighed. "I had hoped that the rumors about Aunt Melody had died down. But when I heard the story again at your party, it made me sad. My great-aunt was a dear, sweet woman, but she was a loner. People who didn't understand her made up stories about her."

She gave Missy a serious look. "I wanted to put an end to the legend of Old Lady Rochester, once and for all."

Missy felt sorry for old Mrs. Rochester. Like Missy and Baby, Melody's great-aunt had gotten a reputation she didn't deserve. Suddenly Missy got an idea. "Maybe we can still do that!" she said.

"What do you mean?" Melody asked.

Missy jumped up. "Let's show Stephanie, Emily, and Willie what a real haunted house is like! After tonight, they won't have the nerve to say mean things about your great-aunt!"

Excited, Missy skipped down the stairs.

"First," Missy said, "we have to fix the door."

Melody showed her the trick to opening the old wooden door. "It always sticks," she explained.

"Second, Baby and I need disguises." She remembered the ghostly sheets in the library.

"I've got an idea," Missy said, going into the room to grab a sheet.

Melody followed her into the room, then stopped. "You found the secret passage!"

Missy looked over at the open bookcase. "Baby was really the one who discovered it."

"How wonderful!" Melody exclaimed, patting Baby on the head. "I've been trying to find this for months. Aunt Melody used to let me play with it when I was little, but I couldn't remember how to get it open."

Missy showed Melody the fake red book that made the door spring open.

"This will save us a lot of money when we restore the house. Now we won't have to rip down walls to find the hidden staircase! Thank you, Missy. And Baby too."

Cheerfully Baby scampered in a circle around the red-haired woman.

Melody laughed. "Your dog is very brave to have run up that dark staircase. He came right up to me—and howled at my flute!"

Missy laughed. "For some reason, your flute playing made Baby go crazy!"

"Thank goodness he's not a music critic!" Melody said. "Now . . . let's get on with your plan . . . before the midnight hour ends!"

A small ghostly figure waited just inside the front door of the Rochester house. It was Melissa Fremont. Melody had cut two holes so Missy could see from beneath the white sheet.

The front door was wide open. Missy kept peeking out from the dark doorway, watching for her friends.

Beside her, Baby was also wearing a sheet. Melody had removed the section covering his face so he could see and breathe.

"Here they come!" Missy told her dog. "Go warn Melody!"

Baby ran up the stairs, the white sheet flying behind him.

When the girls reached the sagging front stairs, Missy stepped into the dark doorway.

Fiddling under the sheet, she tucked her flashlight under her chin then turned it on. Melody had shown her how to aim the light to create an eerie effect, making her face turn a sickly yellow.

Outside, the girls gasped. The ghoulish figure in the doorway was a stark white shape. It had sunken eye sockets and a bony reddish-yellow head that flowed.

"M-M-Missy? Is that you?" asked Emily.

"Something terrible has happened," Willie whispered.

Even Stephanie seemed frightened. "Wh-who are you?" she demanded in a thin voice. "Where's Missy?"

Missy rocked back and forth in the doorway. The long sheet swayed around her ankles. "*I am the ghost of Melissa Fremont,*" she said in a low, spooky voice.

"Aaaah!" the girls squealed, huddling together.

"P-please don't hurt us!" Emily begged.

"What d-do you want from us?" Willie asked.

Still swaying, Missy took a step forward onto the porch. *"I want only one of you. The one who spread nasty stories about old Mrs. Rochester! The one who tried to play dirty tricks on Melissa and Baby!"* As Missy rocked back and forth, the swollen planks creaked under her feet.

"What is it talking about?" Emily whispered, nervously biting her lip.

"I don't know." Willie swallowed hard, trying to hold back her fear.

Stephanie didn't say a word. Her face was pale now, frozen with panic.

Lightning lit the sky, followed by an angry crash of thunder.

"Oh, no!" Emily pulled her jacket closed. "We're really in trouble now!"

"It's just like all those horror movies," Willie shouted. "When the evil spirits use the forces of nature to capture their victims!"

Thunder crackled, rumbling over the earth.

A freak thunderstorm! Missy thought. Even the weather is helping us!

"Let's get out of here!" Emily shrieked.

"Do not go!" Missy lurched forward. *"For I will follow you to the ends of the earth. I will haunt you forever—always—until I find the one I seek!"*

A gust of wind whipped through the air, rippling Missy's sheet. As the girls watched in horror, the ghostly image twisted and danced.

''It's ch-changing shapes,'' Willie said with a shiver.

White lightning sizzled overhead.

"It's getting closer!" Emily wailed, scrambling backward. She tripped over a crack in the sidewalk and stumbled, landing in a patch of tall weeds.

"Come on!" Willie screamed. She grabbed Stephanie's arm, trying to shake some life into her. "Do something!"

Stephanie's eyes were popping with fright as she stared at the wavering ghost. She tried to speak, but her lips were stiff and frozen. "Aaah . . ."

"Come on!" Willie repeated. "You got us into this mess!" She gave Stephanie a shove, but the petrified girl just shook her head.

"Oh," Emily whimpered. "I never wanted to come here! Missy's turned into a ghost—and *we* could be next!"

"No!" Willie shouted, picking Emily up and dragging her limp form across the lawn. "I—you—we—oh!" She gritted her teeth and dared to look back at the ghost. "What do you want from us?"

Once again the sky seemed to explode overhead. Missy let out a shrill laugh in unison with the crackle of thunder. *"I want only one of you. The one who tricked me."* She lifted her hand to point, and her finger made a bony impression in the sheet. *"I have come for STEPHANIE COOK!"*

The three girls screamed, stumbling backward.

A haunting song pierced the air. Right on cue, Melody had started to play the flute. When Missy heard the music floating through the old house, she started to giggle.

The girls looked up, their mouths dropping open in horror. The figure in the upstairs window was too horrible, too real.

It was the ghost of old Mrs. Rochester!

Framed by the window, she was surrounded by fat wax candles. The flickering flames lit her wild red hair, which glowed in a copper halo around her head.

"It's her!" Emily cried.

"She's real! She's alive!" Willie gave Stephanie another shake. "Mrs. Rochester's staring at us!"

The most hideous thing was her eyes. They were enormous bloodshot saucers with an evil glare. Piercing, probing, cutting, those eyes seemed to have the power to see inside a person.

Stephanie lurched backward. "I—I'm getting out of here!" she croaked.

"Wait a minute!" Willie said, holding on to her arm.

"You can't leave!" Emily protested, grabbing Stephanie's other hand.

"*Do not try to escape!*" Missy growled.

"The ghost wants you," Emily said.

"Talk to it!" Willie ordered. "I'm not going to have that creepy thing chasing me around for the rest of my life!"

"No!" Stephanie protested. She tried to break away, but Emily and Willie held her arms tightly. "I—I can't. I want to go home. Let me go!"

The black sky seemed to open up above them with a roar and an electric white flash. Raindrops began to pelt the girls' heads and faces.

"Let go! I want to go home!" Stephanie wailed. Her feet flailed against the ground. "We're getting all wet!"

But the other girls wouldn't let her go. "Don't be a big baby!" Willie said, even though the sight of Mrs. Rochester made her want to run too.

"Come to me!" Missy ordered in a gravelly voice. *"Come to me, Stephanie Cook!"*

"No! Never!" Stephanie whimpered. Driven by fright, she twisted free and ran across the lawn. At the edge of the yard she panicked and dove into the thorny hedges.

"You can run, but you can't hide!" Missy warned.

"Come back here, Stephanie Cook!" Willie shouted, chasing after the frantic girl.

Missy backed into the house, then doubled over in laughter. Baby joined her, wagging his tail.

Still playing her flute, Melody came down the stairs.

"I guess they've had enough," Missy said with a smile. "Why don't you go round them up?" she told her sheepdog.

Baby darted out the door, howling and barking.

"Aaah!" the girls shrieked again when they saw Baby dressed like a ghost.

Missy and Melody burst into laughter.

"It's okay, you guys," Missy called out the door. She pulled off the sheet and smiled at her friends. "It was only me."

Melody shook Missy's hand and winked. "Good show! You and Baby are fine performers."

"Thanks." Missy smiled, happy that her night in the haunted house had turned out to be so much fun.

By the time the girls got inside the house, they were soaked. Missy introduced Melody Rochester Smith, who explained everything to the girls.

"But my little trick on Stephanie backfired when Missy turned up instead," Melody finished.

"Stephanie Cook, how could you be so mean to Missy!" Emily demanded.

Stephanie didn't answer. She just kept staring at the floor.

"But we're all guilty," Willie admitted. "We all spread stories about old Mrs. Rochester."

"Only Missy and Baby didn't believe them. And they had the courage to stand up for their beliefs," Melody added.

"But I can't believe Baby was such a hero tonight," Stephanie told Melody. "You should have seen him in the park when he met my

cousin's dog. He whined and rolled around on the ground like a wimpy coward."

"Oh, really?" Melody asked thoughtfully. "And I bet your cousin's dog is a female, right?"

"Fifi? Oh, she's a perfect lady," Stephanie agreed.

Melody laughed. "Baby wasn't afraid of her! That's just the way male dogs act when they meet female dogs."

"So Baby isn't a scaredy-cat after all!" Emily exclaimed.

Missy gave her dog a big hug. He'd always been her hero, but it was nice for *everyone* to know that he wasn't a chicken.

Suddenly there was a strange rattling sound coming from the front porch.

"What's that?" Emily asked nervously.

"We've learned our lesson," Willie insisted. "Please, no more tricks."

Missy looked at Melody, who shrugged. "I really don't know what it is," Melody said.

Stephanie was in a panic. "I'm getting out of here!" she cried, running down the hall and throwing open the kitchen door.

"Aaah!" she squealed when the skeleton dangled in her face.

Quickly she slammed the kitchen door and opened the one beside it. A sack of flour exploded over her head, covering her with fine white dust.

"Hmmm." Melody seemed confused. "That wasn't one of my tricks."

"It was one of mine," Stephanie admitted from the cloud of white powder. "I rigged it up this afternoon."

The rattling sound grew louder. A minute later Peter danced into the house, jumping up and down, shaking his plastic piggy bank.

"Pennies, pennies, love those pennies!" he sang. He was soaked from the rain.

"Oh, *PeeWee*!" Stephanie groaned. "This is all your fault! If you hadn't scared me like that, I wouldn't have—"

"Run into your own trap?" Willie said.

"Who's the chicken now?" Emily asked.

Baby barked as if he enjoyed the joke too.

Peter looked at his flour-coated cousin and giggled. "Stephanie's a ghost," he said. "Boo!"

"That's true," Melody said. "Stephanie's the only ghost in this haunted house."

"And Missy and Baby are the heroes of Hills Point School," Emily proclaimed.

With a big smile Missy patted her dog on the head. *I don't believe in ghosts,* she thought. At least, until next Halloween!